"What's the point of skating if you don't have fun? You've got to go where the board takes you, even in a strange city. No . . . *especially* in a strange city!"

RYAN BARNES
Age: 13
Hometown: Milwaukee, WI

STONE ARCH BOOKS
presents

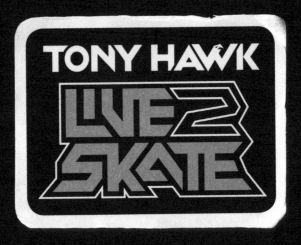

TONY HAWK
LIVE 2 SKATE

AT LARGE

written by
MICHAEL A. STEELE

images by
FERNANDO CANO AND JOE AZPEYTIA

a
CAPSTONE
production

Published by Stone Arch Books
A Capstone Imprint
1710 Roe Crest Drive, North Mankato, Minnesota 56003
www.capstonepub.com • www.capstoneyoungreaders.com

Library of Congress Cataloging-in-Publication Data is
available on the Library of Congress website.
Hardcover: 978-1-4342-4087-3
Paperback: 978-1-4342-6189-2

Summary: Ryan Barnes travels to Argentina with his skate
crew. When he sneaks out after dark, he finds himself in a
different world: a world of trouble.

Editor: Julie Gassman
Editorial Director: Michael Dahl
Designer: Bob Lentz
Creative Director: Heather Kindseth

Design Elements: Shutterstock.

CHAPTERS

STICKING THE TRICK

Ryan Barnes pushed down the roll-in. He crouched, gained speed, and zipped into the skatepark's plaza. Smiling, he aimed for a short set of stairs leading to the lower level. He ollied into the air and performed a frontside 180. Looking over his shoulder, he headed for the stair's metal handrail.

Grind time, Ryan thought as he landed on the rail. He slid down the metal pipe, balancing on the two metal trucks that held each set of wheels. A perfect switch 50-50 grind.

At the end of the rail, Ryan ollied once more, did another 180, and stuck the landing. There was applause and encouraging whistles from the crowd. Skaters banged their boards against the ground in approval.

Ryan was pleased, but he knew he could do better.

It was Ryan's first run of the skating demonstration, and he was determined to impress. At thirteen, he was the youngest member of the Grendel Grind Gear skate team. Ryan was determined to show everyone why someone so young was chosen for the G-3 Crew.

He ollied onto a long grind box, landing in a manual by balancing on just the back wheels. After a couple of feet on the box, he popped up and came down on just the front wheels for a nose manual. When Ryan reached the end, he popped in a clean nollie flip off the box for a perfect landing.

Thirteen-year-old pro skaters weren't unheard of. There were more young skaters with sick skills rolling onto the scene every day. Many of these groms, as they were called, were sponsored by skate shops and gear companies just like Ryan was. But very few got to go on a cool international tour to Argentina. Luckily for Ryan, he was able to go because his nineteen-year-old brother, Josh, was on the G-3 Crew, too.

They began their South American tour at one of the public skateparks in Buenos Aires — Centro Cinco. It was a small park set up in the plaza style for street skating.

The park's obstacles mimicked some of the ones a skater would find in the real world: stairs, long benches, curved concrete planters, and so on.

Ryan smiled as he carved up the quarterpipe. He spotted Shane Wilson crouched at the top. His teammate held out his small video camera. It was perfect timing. Ryan's confidence was up and it showed. He held up two fingers to the camera in a peace sign as his board nosegrinded across the top. He hoped that would make a good shot for his crew's next video.

"Sick!" Shane shouted, obviously pleased with the shot.

Ryan picked up speed as he raced for the cement pyramid. Rolling up one side, he caught air, and did a pop shuvit. The board spun a 180 beneath his feet. Another solid landing. This brought more cheers and applause.

Manuals usually impressed crowds, and they were Ryan's specialty. From the day his brother had showed him one, Ryan seemed to be a natural at balancing on one set of wheels or the other. Alone, they were mildly impressive. But during a line of tricks, manuals always made the tricks look more difficult then they were.

So far, Ryan had stuck every trick. He thought for certain he could pull off the 360 flip with a manual landing. He had only completed the trick a couple of times. In fact, the first time had been an accident. But that was all it took to make him keep trying.

That's the way it was with most skating tricks. After a skater landed one the first time, they got addicted. They had to do it again and again until they could do the trick perfectly. The team's unofficial leader, Sebastian Perez, didn't like any of them to try a new trick in competition until they could stick it *every* time in practice. Ryan was far from sticking this trick every time, but he was having such a great run, he knew he had it in him.

Ryan flew back up the quarterpipe. No hang time at the top this time, he simply rolled back down the ramp. He needed to build some speed. He chanced a glance into the audience and happened to lock eyes with Sebastian. As if reading his mind, Sebastian glared at him and shook his head ever so slightly. Ryan let his eyes move past him and over the crowd. His smile disappeared as his lips tightened.

I don't care what he thinks, thought Ryan. *I'm going for it!*

Ryan ollied onto the grind box for some height. Then, as he reached the end, he ollied again, this time flicking the board with his front foot. His legs spread wide as the board spun completely around and flipped at the same time. When the board leveled out, he planted his feet on the deck, pushing down with his front foot. Unfortunately, as soon as he was in position, he could tell it was all wrong.

He was going to slam.

BRING YOUR GAME

Ryan tried to recover. As his front wheels hit, he tried to land normally — on all four wheels. Too late! His momentum carried him forward, over the board, and toward the hard cement. Ryan resisted the urge to straighten his arms. Instead, he brought them closer to his body and rolled across the pavement. It was just as his brother had taught him years ago. The move was so much a part of him that he heard his brother's voice every time he wiped out.

"If you're going to learn to skate," Josh had said, "then you have to learn how to fall."

The crowd gave a collective moan. Ryan did his best to ignore them along with his new bruises and scrapes.

He quickly picked up his board and aimed it toward the other end of the plaza. He tossed it ahead of him and hopped on, skating back toward his crew.

"Good job, dude," said Shane. He slapped Ryan on the shoulder as Ryan took his helmet off. "Almost a perfect run." His turn to skate, Shane tucked his curly brown bangs into his helmet and leaped onto his board. He rolled in amongst the obstacles.

"You got a little cocky at the end there, but you did good," Josh told him. He tousled Ryan's long blond hair.

"Thanks," Ryan replied.

Sebastian pushed through the nearby spectators. He zeroed in on Ryan. "You just *had* to go for it, didn't you?" His anger seemed to make his accent thicker.

"So? What's the big deal?" Ryan asked.

Sebastian stroked his goatee. "The deal was that I told you to only do the tricks you can stick."

"Come on," said Josh. "Lighten up. It was a good run."

Sebastian pointed at Josh. "Aren't you supposed to babysit him? Make sure he does what he's told? I told you he was too young for the team."

Ryan didn't like being put down in front of everyone. Another time he might have shown the older skater more respect. Now, he just pushed back even harder.

Josh opened his mouth to protest, but Ryan beat him to it. "Who died and left you in charge?" Ryan asked.

"Hey, I built this crew," Sebastian replied. "We wouldn't even be on this tour if it wasn't for me. Don't forget that."

Ryan knew this was all true. Sebastian was big in Buenos Aires, and when he came to the United States, Grendel Grind Gear scrambled to sponsor him. Normally, all that attention didn't seem to go to Sebastian's head. However, ever since they had flown into Argentina, he'd seemed on edge.

"I thought I had it," Ryan said through a clenched jaw. "Besides, everybody makes mistakes."

"Not on this trip," Sebastian replied. "If your game isn't a hundred percent then don't bring it."

Ryan sighed. What was the point of skating if you couldn't have fun? Go where the board takes you. That's what he always enjoyed about skating.

Ryan was about to say this when Sebastian's name was called by the announcer. Their team leader threw down his

board and hopped on. He pushed into the skatepark plaza just as Shane skated in.

Ryan felt a hand on his shoulder. "Okay, dial it down a notch," said Josh. "You . . . we should cut Sebastian some slack."

Ryan glared at his older brother. "That guy's been on my case ever since we got here."

"I think he's just nervous," Josh explained. "He's the hometown hero to some of these guys." He nodded at the crowd. "Got to be a lot of pressure, you know?"

Ryan watched as Sebastian zipped up the quarterpipe. The older skater wore a determined expression as he caught air with a backside 360. He twisted in a complete circle before landing. Not an easy trick on a quarterpipe. Then Sebastian headed for the steps.

He didn't grind the handrail. Instead, he ollied into a 360 flip. The board spun around and flipped over under his outstretched legs. He stuck the landing perfectly and pushed toward the opposite roll in. On the way back, he nollied toward the grind box. The nose-ollie set him up for a perfect crooked grind. He landed in front of the pyramid. He had enough momentum to grind all the way across and come off fakie.

With each trick, the crowd clapped and cheered — more than for any other member of their crew. Sebastian really was a local hero.

Sebastian finished his run with a killer 360 flip off the quarterpipe, a nosegrind off the edge of the grind box, and a primo slide to a stop in the center of the plaza. The slide was particularly impressive, because Sebastian stood on the edge of his board as it scraped along its side. He must have slid six feet before coming to a stop. This brought cheers from the crowd.

Sebastian cracked a relieved smile as he waved a hand to the audience. He popped down and skated back to his teammates.

Sebastian's eyes were on Ryan as he rolled closer. The anger and frustration was gone from his face. Was he going to apologize? He opened his mouth to speak.

"*¿Qué pasa, Seba?*" asked a voice behind Ryan.

Sebastian's smile vanished.

Ryan and his crew turned to see a small group pushing through the crowd. They were led by a tall, thin guy with a buzz cut and a tribal tattoo peeking out from under his shirt collar.

"*Nada*, Arsenio," replied Sebastian. "*¿Cómo estás?*"

"Bien, bien," answered Arsenio as he shook hands with Sebastian and pulled him into a hug.

The two continued their conversation in Spanish, and Ryan was lost. He had picked up enough to understand their greetings: *What's happening? Not much. How are you? Good, good.* But that was it. To understand more, he'd have to fish the Spanish phrasebook out of his backpack. And even then, the two guys spoke so fast Ryan knew he wouldn't be able to look up anything in time.

Finally, Sebastian turned to the rest of the team. "This is my crew," he said. "Ryan, Shane, and Josh." They each nodded in turn.

Arsenio jutted a thumb over his shoulder toward the two guys and girl that followed him. "*Mi amigos*," said Arsenio. "Victor, Mateo, and Aleta."

Victor was short and wore a yellow ball cap cocked to the side. Blades of spiked brown hair jutted up in front. Mateo was as tall as Arsenio and had greasy brown bangs covering most of his eyes. Aleta was thin with straight brown hair with many strands dyed hot pink. They each held a skateboard, and there wasn't a smile between them. That is, except for Arsenio. A thin smile stretched across his face as his wide eyes seemed to feast on the visiting skaters.

"That was a good run, Seba," Arsenio told Sebastian. "It's good to know that you still remember what I taught you."

"It's no problem remembering the easy tricks," Sebastian jabbed. Arsenio laughed and clamped Sebastian on the shoulder.

"We have to party tonight, eh?" he said. "Celebrate your return." Ryan exchanged a glance with Shane. That sounded way cool.

"No, thanks," Sebastian replied. "We have to stay on point for the competition tomorrow."

The full competition would start tomorrow at the Centro Cinco skatepark. Ever since skateboarding had taken off in Argentina, the city government had been great about building public skateparks all over the city. However, there still wasn't one in the barrio where Sebastian grew up. He had pushed for the team to hold a competition in the closest skatepark to help raise money for the new park. If they could raise half the funds, the city would kick in the other half for the skatepark. If Sebastian was serious about skating before, he was doubly serious about the competition.

"You sure?" asked Arsenio. "Remember all the places to street skate? We've found plenty more since you left."

"This one place," Mateo added, "is *very* good."

Arsenio turned to Ryan and the others. "Yes, it would be fun to show you how we skate down here at the bottom of the world."

Shane began to speak, but Sebastian shot him a look. Shane's mouth snapped shut. Both Shane and Ryan loved street skating. Skateparks were great to practice tricks because you really got to know all the obstacles. That all changed with street skating. A skater never knew what he would come across. He might stick the biggest trick off a dumpster that he'd never see again.

Ryan raised an eyebrow at Sebastian. "Really?" He was still ticked from Sebastian's earlier rant. "We come all the way down here and we can't explore the city?"

"*After* the competition," Sebastian replied. "You're no good to us if you break an arm on the street."

Arsenio chuckled. "We'll take good care of your *amigos*," he said.

Josh nudged Ryan. "Remember, if anyone from our team wins, we're donating the prize money to the new park," he added. "It's important that we're *all* at our best."

"You don't have to worry about that," said Mateo. "Our team is the best anyway."

Sebastian smiled. "We'll see."

"So, tomorrow then," said Arsenio.

Sebastian nodded and walked toward the crowd. There were eager young boys and girls waiting for autographs. They had everything from skate magazines to skateboards for him to sign.

As Ryan followed Josh and Shane, he saw Arsenio give a slight snarl in Sebastian's direction. Then the older boy caught Ryan's eye and grinned down at him before turning away.

Ryan picked up his board and began to follow when he felt a tap on his shoulder. It was Aleta.

"Take," she said, holding out a folded piece of paper. "If you change your mind, meet tonight at 10:00."

As Aleta went after her friends, Ryan opened the slip of paper and smiled. *Cool*, he thought. An address was scribbled inside.

"You *know* I'm in," Shane said when Ryan told him about the invitation. It was after dinner and the G-3 Crew had returned to their hotel rooms. Ryan and Shane shared a room while the oldest members of the team, Sebastian and Josh, shared one across the hall.

"We'll wait as long as we can to make sure they're asleep," said Ryan.

As soon as they got back to their room, Ryan used his laptop to find the address. Luckily, their destination wasn't too far from their hotel. And the route had only a couple of turns — very easy.

Usually on tours, if the team didn't go out and explore the town, they would stay in, order pizza, and watch a movie. *Pizza was everywhere,* thought Ryan. *Even five thousand miles from home.*

That night, however, Sebastian insisted they crash early so they'd be at their best for the competition.

Ryan and Shane waited until just after nine thirty. Ryan shoved his Spanish phrasebook into his back pocket and grabbed his board. Shane carefully pulled the door open and glanced down the hallway. "Cool," Shane whispered and slipped outside.

Ryan slinked out after him. He eased the door shut so it wouldn't alert his brother across the hall. Silently, they made their way down to the stairs. Soon, they were speeding down the sidewalk away from the hotel.

Ryan knew being out in a strange city at night was a bad idea. But their hotel was in a nice part of town, and he was with Shane, who was seventeen. It wasn't like they would be alone. They were going to meet Sebastian's friend who knew the city well. Besides, Ryan was still upset at Sebastian and Josh from earlier.

They skidded to a stop at an intersection. "Where to?" asked Shane.

Ryan examined his palm where he had drawn the simple map. "Cross here and take the next left."

The cool night air felt great as they skated down the sidewalk. They laughed as they ollied over the occasional hazard. Shane even did a nosegrind off the front of a long cement bench.

They turned the last corner, and Ryan checked his map again. They had to be close. However, they slowed to a stop when they found the sidewalk full. Dozens of dressed-up people waited to get into a nightclub. An excitement filled the air along with the thumping base line from the music inside.

"Is this the place?" asked Shane.

Ryan checked his hand again. The address matched the brightly painted numbers over the club. "Yup," Ryan replied.

Shane shook his head. "Dude, sneaking out is one thing, but I'm not feelin' this."

Ryan pointed to himself. "We're overdressed, too," he joked. They both wore T-shirts, jeans — with a few holes here and there — and their skating shoes.

"True." Shane laughed. "Let's head back. Maybe we can find some more spots for tricks along the way."

"Cool," Ryan agreed.

They had just turned and dropped their boards when a girl's voice cut through the noise.

"Hey!" she said.

Shane and Ryan turned in unison. Aleta and Victor walked around the large crowd. They each held skateboards and weren't dressed to get into the club either.

"Good, you came," said Aleta.

"So, we're not going in?" Ryan asked, pointing to the club entrance.

Aleta cocked her head. She didn't understand.

"The club," Shane added.

Aleta and Victor exchanged a puzzled look. It was clear that they spoke very little English.

Ryan remembered the dictionary and fished it out of his pocket. He had opened it and was thumbing toward the C section for *club* when it was snatched from his hands. Aleta looked it over and then shook her head.

"You no need," she said with a laugh. Then she put the

book in her pocket, tossed down her board, and skated down the sidewalk. Victor was right behind her.

"Hey," shouted Ryan. He and Shane skated after them.

Aleta led them around to the back of the club and stopped. Once they had caught up with her and Victor, Ryan realized why she had them meet here. The back of the club had a loading dock with a long ramp. One could begin on the ramp, get enough speed, and jump off the loading dock. But that wasn't the best part. The street behind the club sloped away. The way the area was built, the street was like a giant roll-in for the city.

"*¿Bueno, sí?*" asked Victor. Then he pushed off and zoomed up the ramp. When he hit the edge of the loading dock, he performed an 360 ollie, where he scooped the board with his back foot and spun in a complete circle without grabbing.

Aleta followed after with a backside 180. The two stuck their landings and continued skating down the sidewalk. They didn't look back.

Shane raised a hand for a high five. "True street skating, my friend. No looking back. No do-overs."

Ryan high-fived Shane, and the older kid ran up the ramp and hopped onto his board. He shot off the loading dock with a yell and a 180. He landed and continued down the sidewalk.

Ryan followed him with a backside 180 of his own. He couldn't help but smile as he sailed through the air.

BUENA ONDA

Ryan kickflipped onto the curb, then ollied over a large crack in the pavement. Aleta zipped in front of him and ollied up to perform a brief nosegrind on the edge of a short retaining wall. They cut across the street, and Shane pulled a clean boardslide down a handrail. Victor had great board control. While zipping down the rough streets, he could do three or five pop shuvits in a row.

The four skaters tore down the sidewalks of Buenos Aires. Ryan was surprised to see so many other groups of skaters out. Sebastian had told them how quickly skating had caught on in Argentina. Now Ryan could see for himself. Aleta and Victor waved and stopped to chat with many of the other skaters. But they never spoke long. Ryan and Shane's street skating tour guides continued to lead them through the city. Ryan wondered when they would reach that special place Arsenio mentioned at the skatepark.

"Where is Arsenio?" asked Ryan. "And that other guy? Mateo, right?"

"They meet us," Victor replied.

When they finally reached their destination, it was obvious. The group turned a corner and saw a large business park. A huge plaza was sprawled between three tall office buildings. Everything was made of polished granite. The plaza had many levels with several steps and stone handrails. Long stone benches and huge planters were sprinkled about. The sides of the planters curved up into almost perfect quarterpipes. Lights flooded the area so it looked like a pocket of daylight in the middle of the city. Best of all, they had the entire place to themselves.

Victor nodded his head. "*Buena onda*," he said.

Ryan exchanged a look with Shane and then shrugged.

Aleta looked up, thinking, then said, "Eh . . . good vibrations."

Shane nodded in agreement. "Oh, yeah. He's got that right."

"Awesome," said Ryan. He and Shane bumped fists before rolling in.

The skaters split up and spread out. Ryan aimed for one of the long benches. He ollied onto it, landing in a back manual. When he reached the end, he spun a 180 before landing.

"Check it!" shouted Shane. He carved up the side of one of the huge planters. Then he shot off the top with an indy 360, catching big air.

"Sick!" said Ryan. He pushed toward the planter and copied the trick.

He and Shane went back to the planter a few more times. Each time, trying a different trick as they caught air.

"Hey!" shouted Aleta. She gestured for them to follow.

She led them deeper into the plaza where Victor was zooming toward the stairs. The kid ollied up, sailed over the steps, made a 180, and landed on the level below. Aleta followed, but she chose to grind down the stone handrail.

Ryan and Shane were neck and neck. They ollied off the top step together. Ryan popped a melon grab while Shane

performed a method air. He grabbed his board with one hand and pulled it back behind him, his feet still on the deck. His other arm stretched wide. It wasn't perfect — and his landing was a little sketchy — but it still looked great.

"Dude, why aren't all the skaters here?" Shane asked when he landed next to Ryan.

"No idea," Ryan replied. He turned to ask Aleta, but she and Victor had cut away to tackle some of the benches and planters on that level.

"Check it out!" said Shane as he pointed to another set of stairs. They led down into what looked like a large bowl. Shane grinned. "Going down?" He pushed his board toward the steps.

Shane didn't get enough speed to catch as much air as last time. He ollied up and sailed over the stairs with a 180. Ryan followed him with a boardslide down the stone handrail. When he reached the bottom he landed with a nose wheelie. A little sketchy, he stretched his arms as he balanced on his front wheels.

Ryan slid to a stop and looked around. They were at the bottom of some kind of mini amphitheater. Steps and rails covered the bowl surrounding them. It looked as if it were a cool place for people to hang out and chat. One thing was for sure: there was no way to skate out. They'd have to climb the stairs carrying their boards.

"Let's try that again," said Shane.

Ryan popped up his board and caught it with one hand. "Sure."

"*Hey!*" said a deep voice from above. "*Hey, ustedes!*"

Two older men stood at the top of the bowl. They each wore tan shirts and ties. There was no mistaking it. They were security guards.

"Oh, man," said Shane.

Ryan couldn't understand what the men said, but the meaning was clear. The closest guard gestured for them to climb the steps.

When the boys reached the top, they saw that there were four security guards in all. Two golf carts were parked nearby. Ryan looked around for their guides, and hopefully, interpreters. But Aleta and Victor were gone.

"Just be cool," Josh had told him. "Always talk respectfully to cops or security guards."

Early on, Ryan's brother had taught him how to talk to officers. Skaters got a bad reputation sometimes. Many authority figures were already on edge, with their minds made up.

"Don't make any wild moves or raise your voice," Josh had advised. "Just tell them you're sorry and that you'll leave."

Unfortunately, there was a big problem with Josh's advice at the moment.

"¿*Habla inglés?*" Ryan asked. It was one of the few Spanish phrases he knew. He had asked if they spoke English. Unfortunately, they all shook their heads.

"We're sorry," Shane said, almost yelling. "We didn't know."

Ryan shook his head. "Dude, talking louder won't help."

He eased his hand toward his back pocket, going for his phrasebook. As soon as he felt the empty pocket, he remembered that Aleta still had it. Unfortunately, both she and Victor were nowhere to be found.

The four men continued to speak in Spanish, both to the kids and each other. Ryan and Shane just shrugged their shoulders.

"What should we do?" Ryan asked.

"Let's just try to go," replied Shane. He picked up his board and took a step back. "We're just going to go now," he told the guards.

That really stirred them up. The closest guard grabbed Shane by the arm.

"Hey, man," said Shane. "It's cool. We just want to get out of your hair."

None of the security guards looked sympathetic. Ryan couldn't understand them, but it was clear that they were deciding what to do with them. Would they call the police? Ryan didn't even know the laws in Argentina. Could they arrest them for trespassing? The last place he wanted to be was in jail — in another country.

Another guard spoke to someone on his radio. A third security guard reached into one of the golf carts and pulled out something Ryan didn't like seeing — two long, plastic wrist restraints.

"Dude, we gotta bolt," said Ryan. "Seriously."

Shane's eyes widened. "I'm with you," he said. "Get ready."

Suddenly, Shane wrenched his arm from the security guard's grasp. The older boy took off running.

Ryan barely gave himself a chance to think. He threw his board to the ground, sending it rolling ahead of him. He ran after it, hopped onto the deck, and pushed as hard as he could. He felt hands snatch at his shirt, but none of them took hold.

Ryan glanced back to see one guard running after him. Shane still held his own board and pulled away from his pursuer. He angled toward Ryan. Unfortunately, the other guards had hopped into the golf carts and were in pursuit. Their electric motors whirred as they closed the gap.

Shane pointed ahead to the sets of stairs. Ryan changed course, and he and Shane converged on them. Ryan jumped to the ground and scooped up his board. He and Shane hit the steps and leaped up them two at a time. The guards on foot were still close, but the carts veered away. They must have headed for a ramp to the next level.

Ryan's side began to ache, but he kept his speed. He and Shane headed toward the side of the plaza they had entered. Ryan glanced back and saw the guards slowing down. He threw down his board and hopped on. Shane copied him. They exited the property and skated up the sidewalk. They turned a corner and lost sight of the business park. Both boys stopped pushing and glided along, catching their breath.

"Man, they were going to arrest us," Shane said between quick breaths.

"So, security guards can arrest you here?" asked Ryan.

Shane shook his head, and drops of sweat flew from his damp hair.

Just then, the shrill whirring of electric motors filled the air. Both boys looked back to see the two golf carts zip around the corner — two security guards each. They drove down the city street after them.

7

SKETCHY LANDING

Ryan's eyes widened. He hadn't expected them to follow them out of the business plaza.

"No way!" shouted Shane. He pushed at the ground, gaining speed.

Ryan did the same as they continued up the sidewalk. They carved a sharp left at the next intersection. The gentle downward slope that they had enjoyed on the way to the business park now worked against them. They kept pushing, but they were barely maintaining speed. Meanwhile, the security carts sped around the corner, closer than before. At the rate they were going, they would be better off dumping their boards and running.

"There!" Ryan shouted, pointing to an alley up ahead.

He led the way as they cut right, into the narrow corridor. The good news was that it leveled out enough so they didn't have to work as hard. The bad news was that the alley wasn't narrow enough to keep the golf carts from following them. The carts' tires squealed as they turned in after them.

Ryan and Shane zipped through the alley, crossed the next street, and shot into the next alley. Ryan's chest tightened. A large delivery truck was backed into a loading dock, blocking the way. He looked back. The security guards hadn't given up. They followed the boys into the second alley.

The boys skidded to a stop. Shane's eyes darted back and forth. "Maybe one of these doors is open."

Ryan popped up his board and ran forward. "Follow me."

Although the truck was large, it was a flatbed and too short to slide beneath. It was backed up to the loading dock, and the front of the truck was next to a large, metal dumpster. There was no getting past the front of it. That just left the dock itself.

Ryan sprinted up the stairs running perpendicular to the open loading bay. When he reached the top, he jumped over the handrail and leaped toward the dock itself. He brought his board around and planted his feet on the deck. Workers ducked out of the way, and Ryan landed and moved toward the edge. "Excuse me," he said as he ollied up and grinded down the edge of the dock, past the truck bed. He landed on the alley floor and skidded to a stop. He looked up to see Shane right behind him.

Shane did the same move. But when he ollied off the edge, he pushed off too late and overshot. He landed ahead of his board and tumbled across the alley.

Ryan picked up Shane's board and ran to help him up. "You okay?" asked Ryan.

"Aw, man," Shane groaned. "I twisted my ankle."

Angry voices from the other side of the truck grabbed Ryan's attention. The security guards were saying something to the workers.

"We have to bounce," said Ryan.

He helped Shane to his feet. The older boy cringed when he put weight on his ankle, but he was able to walk on it. So it wasn't broken. But he had a definite limp as they made their way out of the alley.

It was slow going back to the hotel. Not only were they going uphill most of the way, but Shane was in no condition to skate. By the time they returned it was almost midnight. Unfortunately, Sebastian and Josh were waiting for them in the lobby. The night couldn't get any worse.

"Just perfect," said Sebastian. He glared down at the younger boys.

"We just wanted to do some street skating," said Ryan.

"And we ran into a little trouble," Shane added.

"With Arsenio, there's always trouble," said Sebastian.

"Arsenio wasn't even there," Ryan explained. He told them about meeting Aleta and Victor and how they had abandoned them at the business park.

"And now we're down a skater," said Sebastian. He shook his head in disgust. "I hope it was worth it." He headed back upstairs, and Shane slowly limped after him.

Ryan thought about following them, but he knew that wasn't going to happen. Even though he watched Shane and Sebastian walk away, he could feel Josh's angry stare. Ryan plopped down onto one of the lobby couches.

"All right," he said. "Let's get it over with."

Josh sat next to him. "There's nothing to say. You're not stupid. You know what you did was wrong. And you know that we probably lost a team member for tomorrow."

Ryan began to protest but stopped. His brother was right. If he had just torn up that address from Aleta, none of it would've ever happened.

"Mom trusted me to take care of you, and you ditched me," Josh continued.

Ryan sighed. "I know, and I'm sorry, but . . ."

"There's no *buts*, man," Josh shook his head. "You let me down. You let all of us down." Josh stood and walked back to the stairs. "Maybe you're too young to be on this crew."

Ryan flew off the grind box with his third 180, but did a shuvit, simultaneously turning it into a big-spin. He pushed harder toward the stairs. An ollie up to the handrail and a 50-50 grind. Next, he grinded just his front trucks down one edge of the grind box — nosegrind.

Ryan's minute and a half was almost up. He pushed to the quarterpipe and shot up the incline. Leaning to the side, he carved his board across the top of the ramp and finished with a 360. The spectators clapped and the skaters slapped their boards against the ground. Ryan's first round was over.

Centro Cinco was packed. If Sebastian drew the crowds the day before, then the chance to skate against him and take home the prize money was an even bigger draw. Music filled the air as a DJ laid down some killer beats.

Normally, a crowd that size would energize Ryan. He never got stage fright. Instead, he always channeled the crowd's energy into his tricks. But after what had happened the night before, he wasn't psyched about anything. He was worried about getting kicked off the crew. He stuck all his tricks, but his spirit really wasn't in it. He didn't push himself. He kept to the tricks he knew he could stick — just like Sebastian had told him.

Ryan had a lot of time to reflect on the night before. He and his crew didn't have to skate right away because the competition began with the amateurs. They skated in groups of six and were given points for the best tricks. Granted, the tricks weren't complicated, and most of them didn't stick the landings — but what they lacked in skill, they made up in enthusiasm. It wasn't so long ago that Ryan was a newbie, too. Plus, it was cool to watch a few of the young skaters. Some were as young as eight years old. But already, those groms were on their way.

The top three amateur skaters would be allowed to skate

in the next few heats — the intermediates. Likewise, the top three intermediates would get to skate in the final rounds of the day — the advanced category.

The best skaters of all would each get three final rounds to score the most points. The skater with the highest total score would be the winner.

Ryan hadn't paid much attention to the competition so far. His mind kept going back to the previous night. He regretted going out in the first place. He should have just stayed in like Sebastian had instructed. Now Shane was out of commission, and this might be Ryan's last comp with the G-3 crew.

Ryan had yet to run into Arsenio, Aleta, and the others. He wondered if their invitation had just been a setup. Aleta and Victor must have known that they weren't allowed to skate at that business plaza. That's why there weren't any other skaters around. Maybe that was their plan all along. Maybe they wanted to get Shane and Ryan arrested so they wouldn't be able to compete.

When Ryan returned to his team, Shane gave him a fist bump. "Nailed it, dude," he said. He was resting with his bandaged ankle up, but he still held his video camera. "I got some cool shots, too."

"Good job," Josh offered.

"Thanks," Ryan replied.

Sebastian simply gave him a nod. Nothing more.

Ryan sighed and moved to the back of the crowd. The audience was already cheering for the next competitor. Ryan wasn't particularly interested.

Ryan felt a tap on his shoulder. He turned to see Arsenio standing there, grinning. He held out Ryan's phrasebook.

"I heard you did good last night," said Arsenio. "I'm sorry I couldn't be there to see it."

Ryan reached for his book. "Thanks for the setup. We almost went to jail," he said.

Arsenio laughed. "No, you are too talented for that." He tousled Ryan's hair. "Aleta tells me you played your part well. Led those guards on . . . how do you Americans say it? A wild goose chase."

Ryan shrugged off Arsenio's hand and took his book. "Whatever."

"You can skate with us anytime, *cómplice*," said Arsenio.

He raised an eyebrow. "Don't know that word? Look it up in your little book." When Ryan gave him a puzzled look, Arsenio laughed harder. "I have to go skate now. Show Seba how it's done. *Hasta la vista, mi cómplice.*" Arsenio pushed through the crowd toward the skate area.

Cómplice? Ryan thought. He opened the book and thumbed toward the *C* section. He didn't find the definition. Instead, stuffed inside the pages of his book was a stack of Argentinean money. Fifty-peso bills.

Ryan made his way back to his crew just as Arsenio rolled into the plaza. The crowd cheered and banged their boards as he did his first trick. It was a flawless crooked grind down the handrail. Arsenio had perfect balance as the simple nosegrind was made more difficult by angling the tail away from the rail. Then he hit the quarterpipe and caught some air with a frontside 180. Before landing, he added a late shuvit with his front foot. The trick looked particularly impressive because Arsenio spun the board at the end of the trick.

Ryan barely paid attention to Arsenio's tricks. His mind was on the money in his phrasebook. It sat in his front pocket like a brick. Three hundred and fifty pesos. He thought that added up to forty or fifty US dollars. After he had counted out the money, he looked up that word Arsenio called him. The word was *cómplice*. In English, it meant *accomplice*. Had Ryan and Shane helped Arsenio commit a crime? It seemed that he had.

Sebastian nudged Ryan and pointed to Arsenio. "I want you to watch him closely, grom."

Arsenio was almost through with his run. He popped a 360 flip off the pyramid, carved a sharp semicircle, and pushed toward the stairs.

"Arsenio . . . he is a natural," said Sebastian. "It was like he was born with his feet on the deck."

Arsenio flew over the stairs. He slipped his right foot off the board for another late shuvit. This time, the move came so late it didn't look as if the board would come around in time. But it did — just barely. Arsenio bent his knees as he landed.

"He is much better than me," Sebastian admitted.

Ryan frowned. "Then how are you going to win the competition?"

"Oh, I'll win." Sebastian said. "Because I work harder than Arsenio. Arsenio may be better naturally, but he doesn't try to improve or learn new tricks."

Ryan watched Arsenio with a new realization. The skater moved with a confidence that Ryan hadn't noticed before. It really did seem as if the board was a part of his body.

"In the beginning, even though Arsenio taught me how to skate, I was always jealous of his skill." Sebastian shook his head. "I even helped him commit crimes. Sometimes I was the lookout. Sometimes I acted as a distraction."

Ryan caught his breath. "What kind of crimes?"

"Burglaries, mostly," replied Sebastian. "Arsenio and his gang will steal anything and sell it if they get the chance."

The wad of cash in Ryan's pocket felt heavier.

"But that doesn't matter," said Sebastian. "The point is that I could still be a part of that. If I hadn't practiced and worked for a better life, I could be just like Victor, Mateo, or Aleta."

Sebastian took his gaze away from Arsenio. He looked Ryan in the eyes. "That is why I'm so hard on you, grom. You are like Arsenio in some ways."

Cómplice, Ryan thought. His hand moved to his leg. He felt the wad of pesos through his jeans pocket. "I shouldn't have gone out with them last night," he said.

"No," Sebastian agreed. "And you'll pay for it dearly for the rest of the tour."

Ryan looked up. "You mean I get to stay on the crew?"

Sebastian smirked. "I think so. But you may not like it so much." He frowned. "When you're not practicing, you and Shane will be lugging, cleaning, and maintaining all of our gear — no questions asked."

"Okay," Ryan agreed. With all that work, it was going to be a long, hard tour. But at least he got to stay on the crew.

"And if there is any street skating, we do it together," Sebastian added. "No more getting into trouble."

"All right," Ryan agreed. "I won't turn out like Arsenio."

Sebastian's face lightened. "Listen, grom. When I say you are like Aresenio, it's not because you cause trouble. It's because much of skating comes naturally to you. But unlike him, you push yourself. You work hard to perfect new tricks."

"Like my 360 flip manual?" asked Ryan.

"Yes." Sebastian laughed.

"And you know what?" he added. "I shouldn't have kept you from trying that trick."

"Yeah, but you wanted everything perfect for the tour," Ryan said.

"Yes, but I was wrong," Sebastian said. "Look, I'm going to be pushing myself today. I may stumble, but I still plan to win. That is why we will always win. We don't take the easy way out. We push ourselves. We don't settle. We try new things."

Ryan nodded. "That is what skating is all about."

Sebastian smiled. "*Sí, amigo.*"

As Sebastian left to gear up for his run, Ryan made his way toward the plaza. He gazed at the excited spectators and skaters. He felt connected to all of them. Whether they stood on the sidelines or stood on the deck, they all loved the thrill of skating. Ryan remembered why this competition was so important. The new skatepark would give even more kids the chance to feel the same way.

Arsenio performed his last trick and skated toward the spectators. He picked up his board and moved through a crowd boiling with high fives, fist bumps, and handshakes.

Ryan pushed his way toward the older skater. "Good run," Ryan told him when he was close.

"Ah, you were watching," Arsenio replied. "I hope you learned something."

"I did," Ryan replied. He held up the wad of pesos. "Thanks for donating to the new skatepark fund."

Arsenio's grin vanished as Ryan smiled and walked away.

When Arsenio skated his last run, Ryan paid close attention. It was just as Sebastian had said. Aresenio was an awesome skater. He performed every flip, grind, and spin with confidence. The Argentinean rode his board so casually, almost daring himself to fall. No doubt, this was why he scored so high with the judges.

Sebastian was right, though. Arsenio didn't seem to push himself. He didn't stumble and none of his tricks landed sketchy. His execution was perfect because he didn't attempt any trick that he didn't know he could land. It was obvious.

And that was how Sebastian planned to beat him.

The spectators cheered when Sebastian rolled into the plaza. He started strong, launching over the stairs with a 360 flip. Sebastian's legs spread wide before landing back on the board. He carved up the quarterpipe, did a 50-50 across the top, and ollied up into the air. Using the toe of his front foot, he flipped the board once before landing.

The landing was a little sketchy, but Ryan could tell that Sebastian didn't care. At the grind box, Sebastian ollied up into a pop shuvit. He landed on the box and pushed for some more speed. Another ollie into a 360 flip and a perfect landing.

Skaters received more points for harder tricks. Even if Sebastian's tricks weren't as smooth as Aresenio's, they were much more difficult. Just like in skating video games, a long series of tricks could get more points. That was Sebastian's strategy. During his runs, he performed long lines of tricks. Simpler tricks in between the harder ones. He also scored big points when he combined different tricks.

Sebastian's round was almost over. He pushed toward the stairs, boardslid down the handrail, and headed for the quarterpipe. Grabbing his board at the top of the pipe, he spun a slow 180. Then he landed straight down the pipe, gaining speed as he zipped toward the pyramid.

"Pop it, Sebastian!" Ryan cheered. He had a feeling he knew where the skater was going.

Sebastian flew off the top of the pyramid and performed an impossible. The trick was done by kicking the board in such a way that it rotated around the skater's back foot. It was similar to the way someone would twirl a baton. The trick got its name because it truly looks impossible. Sebastian stuck the trick and leveled out just in time for the landing. When he hit, he waved his arms a bit to keep his balance, but he didn't fall.

"Yeah!" Ryan cheered with the crowd. He slapped his board against the cement.

Sebastian's total score was 135.33, beating Arsenio's total score of 101.33. The spectators cheered when the score was announced. Ryan was the last to skate. But since Sebastian's total score was so high, it was clear that he would win the competition. The pressure was off. The prize money would go to the new skatepark.

Ryan stood and popped up his board. He glanced at his crew before rolling into the park.

Shane gave him a thumbs-up. "Pressure's off, dude. Just have fun."

"That's right," Josh agreed. He placed a helmet onto Ryan's head. "And make G-3 proud."

Ryan smiled. He clipped his helmet strap and rolled into the plaza.

The cheers from the crowd finally energized him. He pushed with his foot to gain some speed and rolled straight for the pyramid. An ollie off the top, a smooth 180, and into a big-spin for good measure. The skaters banged their boards and the spectators clapped.

Next, Ryan carved up the side of the quarterpipe with a nosegrind across the lip. He nollied in and landed on the curve of the ramp, pointing straight down. He leaned forward, gaining speed.

This is what skating is all about, Ryan thought. *Being a part of something big but still pushing yourself to the limit.*

When he leveled out, Ryan pushed toward the grind box. He ollied onto it, landing in a nose manual. He rolled a couple of feet and nollied into a frontside shuvit, landing in a regular manual. The spectators cheered.

Ryan felt it. He knew he could pull it off. He chanced a glance to Sebastian. The South American skater sported a slight smile. He slowly nodded his head. Ryan returned the smile as he slammed down the front of his board.

There were only a few feet left on the grind box. Ryan pushed for speed and then ollied off the end. While in midair, he kicked the board around with his front foot. At the same time, he pressed down ever so slightly to make sure the board flipped as well as spun. Ryan's legs spread wide as the board spun and twirled below him. When the deck came back around, he planted his feet on the bolts well before hitting the ground.

As he descended, Ryan pushed his back foot down. With his arms spread wide to keep his balance, the back wheels hit the ground. He kept the nose up and rolled across the plaza on just his back wheels.

He did it! Ryan stuck his 360 flip manual! The crowd roared and the skaters banged their boards. Ryan knew that trick would score him big points. But he also knew that there were other tricks out there. Bigger and better tricks. He was going to keep skating until he could stick them all.

Ryan Barnes still skates with the G-3 Crew. Inspired by his teammate Sebastian, he also volunteers by teaching skate tricks to area kids. They love watching him skate; his signature move

His story has inspired custom skateboard and sticker designs.

L2S At Large

L2S Barnes Hawk Face

L2S Everything's Bueno

SKATE CLINIC:
KICKFLIP

1. Place your back foot across the tail of the skateboard and your front foot between the trucks. Your front foot should be at about a 45-degree angle, with your heel hanging off the edge of the board slightly.

2. Ollie the board into the air. Your ollie only needs to be high enough that the board has room to flip around 360 degrees. As you ollie, slide your front foot up diagonally, flicking it off to the side. This motion starts the board flipping.

3. Pull your knees up, and keep an eye on your board as it flips the full rotation. Lower your feet as the board comes back around, placing your feet over the trunks of the board.

4. Put pressure on the board by straightening your legs. This keeps the board from flipping out from under you.

SKATE CLINIC:
TERMS

50-50 grind
a move where a skater pops up onto an obstacle, then grinds his or her trucks along it

backside 360
a move where the skater and board rotates a full 360 degrees in the air, turning so the back of the skater is on the outside of the rotation's arc

frontside 180
a move where the skater and board rotates 180 degrees so that the body faces frontward when in the air

indy 360
a move where a skater places his or her leading hand on the heel side of the board while turning 360 degrees in the air

kickflip
a move where the rider pops the skateboard into the air and flicks it with the front foot to make it flip all the way around in the air before the skater lands on the board again

manual
a move where a skater balances on their back wheels while rolling along with the front wheels in the air

method air
a move where while in the air, the skater reaches down with his or her back hand and drabs the heel edge of the board between their feet. The skater pulls board toward his or her back, while bending his or her knees.

nosegrind
a move where the skater grinds across the obstacle with only the front truck

pop shuvit
a move where the skater ollies and spins the board 180 degrees before landing on the board again

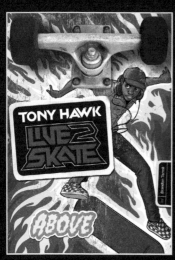

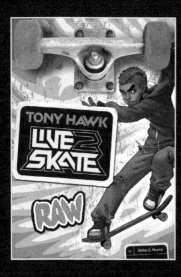

HOW DO YOU LIVE?

written by

MICHAEL A. STEELE

Michael A. Steele has been in the entertainment industry for almost twenty years. He worked in many capacities of film and television production, from props and special effects all the way up to writing and directing. For the past fifteen years, Mr. Steele has written exclusively for family entertainment. For television and video, he wrote for shows including *WISHBONE, Barney & Friends,* and *Boz, The Green Bear Next Door.* He has also authored over sixty books for various characters including Batman, Shrek, Spider-Man, Garfield, G.I. Joe, Speed Racer, Sly Cooper, and The Penguins of Madagascar.

pencils and colors by

FERNANDO CANO

Fernando Cano is an all-around artist living in Monterrey, Mexico, currently working as a concept artist for video game company CGbot. Having published with Marvel, DC, Pathfinder, and IDW, he spends his free time playing video games, singing, writing, and above all, drawing!

inks by

JOE AZPEYTIA

Joe Azpeytia currently lives in Mexico and works as a freelance graphic designer for music bands and international companies. Currently an illustration artist at The Door on the Wall studio, he enjoys playing drums, playing video games, and drawing.